Arthur Sherburne Hardy

Songs of Two

in large print

 MEGALI

Arthur Sherburne Hardy

Songs of Two

in large print

Reproduction of the original.

1st Edition 2024 | ISBN: 978-3-38732-876-9

Megali Verlag is an imprint of Outlook Verlagsgesellschaft mbH.

Verlag (Publisher): Outlook Verlag GmbH, Zeilweg 44, 60439 Frankfurt, Deutschland
Vertretungsberechtigt (Authorized to represent): E. Roepke, Zeilweg 44, 60439 Frankfurt, Deutschland
Druck (Print): Books on Demand GmbH, In de Tarpen 42, 22848 Norderstedt, Deutschland

SONGS OF TWO

BY
ARTHUR SHERBURNE HARDY

1900

SONGS OF TWO

I

Last night I dreamed this dream: That I was dead;
And as I slept, forgot of man and God,
That other dreamless sleep of rest,
I heard a footstep on the sod,
As of one passing overhead,—
And lo, thou, Dear, didst touch me on the breast,
Saying: "What shall I write against thy name
That men should see?"
Then quick the answer came,
"I was beloved of thee."

II

Dear Giver of Thyself when at thy side,
I see the path beyond divide,
Where we must walk alone a little space,
I say: "Now am I strong indeed
To wait with only memory awhile,
Content, until I see thy face,—"
Yet turn, as one in sorest need,
To ask once more thy giving grace,
So, at the last
Of all our partings, when the night

Has hidden from my failing sight
The comfort of thy smile,
My hand shall seek thine own to hold it fast;
Nor wilt thou think for this the heart ingrate,
Less glad for all its past,
Less strong to bear the utmost of its fate.

III

As once through forest shade I went,
I heard a flower call, and bent—
Then strove to go. Should love not spare?
"Nay, Dearest, this is love's sweet share
Of selfishness. For which is best,
To die alone or on thy breast?
If thou hast heard my call,
Take fearlessly, thou art my guest—
To give is all"
Hush! O Love, thou casuist!

IV

Ask me not why,—I only *know*,
It were thy loss if I could show
Thee cause as for a lesser thing.
Remember how we searched the spring,
But found no source,—so clear the sky

4

Within its earth bound depths did lie,
Give to thy joy its wings,
And to thy heart its song, nor try
With questionings
The throbbing throat that sings.

V

  For in thy clear and steadfast eyes
Thine own self wonder deepest lies,
Nor any words that lips can teach
Are sweeter than their wonder speech.
And when thou givest them to me,
Through dawns of tenderness I see,—
As in the water-sky,
The sun of certainly appear.
So, *ask* me why,
For then thou knowest, Dear.

VI

  To give is more than to receive, men say.
But thou hast made them one! What if, some day,
Men bade me render back the gifts I cannot pay,—
Since all were undeserved! should I obey?
Lo, all these years of giving, when we try
To own our thanks, we hear the giver cry;

5

"Nay, it was thou who givest, Dear, not I."
If Wisdom smile, let Wisdom go!
All things above
This is the truest; that we know because we love,
Not love because we know.

VII

Let it not grieve thee, Dear, that Love is sad,
Who, changeless, loveth so the things that change,—
The morning in thine eyes, the dusk within thy hair,
Were it not strange
If he were glad
Who cannot keep thy heart from care,
Or shelter from the whip of pain
The bosom where his head hath lain?
Poor sentinel, that may not guard
The door that love itself unbarred!
Who in the sweetness
Of his service knows its incompleteness,
And while he sings
Of life eternal, feels the coldness of Death's wings.

VIII

Stoop with me, Dearest, to the grass
One little moment ere we pass

6

From out these parched and thirsty lands,
See! all these tiny blades are hands
Stretched supplicating to the sky,
And listen, Dearest, patiently,—
Dost thou not hear them move?
The myriad roots that search, and cry
As hearts do, Love,
"Feed us, or let us die!"

IX

Beloved, when far up the mountain side
We found, almost at eventide,
Our spring, how far we did fear
Lest it should dare the trackless wood
And disappear!
And lost all heart when on the crest we stood
And saw it spent in mist below!
Yet ever surer was its flow,
And, ever gathering to its own
New springs of which we had not known,
To fairer meadows
Swept exultant from the woodland shadows;
And when at last upon the baffling plain
We thought it scattered like a ravelled skein,—
Lo, tranquil, free,
Its longed-for home, the wide unfathomable sea!

7

X

Thy names are like sweet flowers that grow
Within a garden where I go,
Sometimes at dawn, to see each one
Life its head proudly in the sun;
Sometimes at night,
When only by the fragrant air,
I know them there.
And none are grieved or think I slight
Their worth, if closest to my breast,
This one I take which holds within its own
Each single fragrance of the rest,—
My friend, my friend!
And as I loved it first alone,
So shall I love it to the end,
For none were half so dear were it not best.

XI

My every purpose fashioned by some thought of thee,
 Though as a feather's weight that shapes the arrow's flight it
be;
 No single joy complete in which thou hast no fee,
 Though thy share be the star and mine its shadow in the sea;
 Thy very pulse my pulse, thy every prayer my prayer.
 Thy love my blue o'erreaching sky that bounds me
everywhere,—

Yet free, Beloved, free! for this encircling air
I cannot leave behind, doth but love's boundlessness
declare.

XII

    Last night the angel of remembrance brought
Me while I slept—think, Dear! of all his store
Just that one memory I thought
Banished forever from our door!
Thy sob of pain when once I hurt thee sure.
Then in my dream I suddenly was ware
Of God above me saying: "Reach
Thy hand to Me in prayer,
And I will give thee pardon yet."
Thou? Nay, she hath forgiven, teach
Her to forget.

XIII

    Love me not, Dearest, for the smile,
The tender greeting, or the wile
By which, unconscious of its road,
My soul seeks thine in its abode;
Nor say "I love thee of thine eyes,—"
For when Death shuts them, where thy skies?
But love me for my love,

9

Then am I safe from all surprise,
And thou above
The loss of all that dies.

XIV

    Dear hands, forgiving hands,
There is no speech so sure as thing.
Lips falter with so much
To tell, eyes fill with thoughts I scarce divine,
But thy least touch
Soul understands.
Dear giving, taking hands,
There are no gifts so free as thine.
One last gem from the heart of the mine,
One last cup from the veins of the vine,
From the rose to the wind one last sweet breath,
Then poverty, and death!
But thy dear palms
Are richest empty, asking alms.

XV

    A little moment at the end
Of day, left over in the candle light
On the shore of dreams, on the edge of sleep,
Too small to throw away,

10

Too poor to keep!
But it holds two words for thee, dear Friend,—
Good-night, Good night!
And so this remnant of the day,
Left over in the candle-light
On the shore of dreams, on the edge of sleep,
Becomes too great to throw away,
Too dear to keep!

XVI

Beloved, when I read some fine conceit,
Wherein are wrought as in glass
The features love hath made so sweet,
I marvel at so bold an art;
Seeing thou art too dear to praise
Upon the highway where men pass.
For when I seek
To tell the ways
God's hand of tenderness
Hath touched thine earthly part,
Again I hear
Thy first own cry of happiness,
And, sweetest of God's sounds, the dear
Remonstrance of thy giving heart,—
And cannot speak!

XVII

Across the plain of Time
I saw them marching all night long,—
The endless throng
Of all who ever dared to fight with wrong.
All the blood of their hearts, the prime
And crown of their fleeting years,
All the toil of their hands, the tears
Of their eyes, the thought of their brain,
For a word from the lips of Truth,
For a glimpse of the scroll of Fate,
Ere love and youth
Were spent in vain,
And even truth too late!
Oh, when the Silence speaks, and the scroll
Unrolls to the eye of the soul,
What will it be that shall pay the cost
Of the pain gone waste and the labor lost!
And then, Dear, waking, I saw you—-
And knew.

XVIII

We thought when Love at last should come,
The rose would lose its thorn,
And every lip but Joy's be dumb
When Love, sweet Love, was born;

That never tears should start to rise,
No night o'ertake our morn,
Nor any guest of grief surprise,
When Love, sweet Love, was born.

   And when he came, O Heart of mine!
And stood within our door,
No joy our dreaming could divine
Was missing from his store.
The thorns shall wound our hearts again,
But not the fear of yore,
for all the guests of grief and pain
Shall serve him evermore.

XIX

   Dost thou remember, Dear, the day
We met in those bare woods of May?
Each had a secret unconfessed,
Each sound a promise, in each nest.
Young wings a-tremble for the air,—
How we joined hands?—not knowing where
The springs that touch set free
Should find their sea.
Speechless—so sure we were to share
The unknown good to be.

XX

The woods are bare again. There are
No secrets now, the bud's a scar;
No promises,—this is the end!
Ah, Dearest, I have seen thee bend
Above thy flowers as one who knew
The dying wood should bloom anew.
Come, let us sleep, Perchance
God's countenance,
Like thine above thy flowers, smiles through
The night upon us two.

VERSES
MY FRIEND

I have a friend who came,—I know not how,
Nor he. Among the crowd, apart,
I feel the pressure of his hand, and hear
In very truth the beating of his heart.

My soul had shut the door of abode,
So poor it seemed for any guest
To tarry there a night,—until he came,

Asking, not entertainment, only rest.

   Our hands were empty,-his and mine alike,
He says—until they joined. I see
The gifts he brought; but where were mine
That he should say "I too have need of thee?"

   Without the threshold of his heart I wait
Abashed, afraid to enter where
So radiant a company do meet,
Yet enter boldly, knowing I am there.

   Whether his hand shall press my latch to-night,
To-morrow, matters not. He came
Unsummoned, he will come again; and I,
Though dead, shall answer to my name.

   And yet, dear friend, in whom I rest content,
Speak to me *now*—lest when we meet
Where tears and hunger have no grace,
A little word of friendship be less sweet.

ON NE BADINE PAS AVEC LA MORT

1

The dew was full of sun that morn
(Oh I heard the doves in the ladyricks coop!)
As he crossed the meadows beyond the corn,
Watching his falcon in the blue.
How could he hear my song so far,—
The song of the blood where the pulses are!
Straight through the fields he came to me,
(Oh I saw his soul as I saw the dew!)
But I hid my joy that he might not see,
I hid it deep within my breast,
As the starling hides in the maize her nest.

2

Back through the corn he turned again,
(Oh little he cared where his falcon flew!)
And my heart lay still in the hand of pain,
As in winter's hand the rivers do.
How could he hear its secret cry,
The cry of the dove when the cummers die!
Thrice in the maize he turned to me,
(Oh I saw his soul as I saw the dew!)
But I hid my pain that he might not see—
I hid it deep as the grave is made,

Where the heart that can ache no more is laid.

    3

Last night, where grows the river grass,
(Oh the stream was dark though the moon was new!)
I saw white Death with my lover pass,
Side by side as the troopers so.
"Give me," said Death, "thy purse well-filled,
And thy mantle-clasp which the moonbeams gild;
Save the heart which beats for thy dear sake,"
(Oh I saw my heart as I saw the dew!)
"All life hath given is Death's to take."
Dear God! how can I love thy day
If thou takest the heart that loves away!

ITER SUPREMUM

Oh, what a night for a soul to go!
The wind a hawk, and the fields in snow;
No screening cover of leaves in the wood,
Nor a star abroad the way to show.

Do they part in peace, soul with its clay?
Tenant and landlord, what do they say?

Was it sigh of sorrow or of release
I heard just now as the face turned gray?

What if, aghast on the shoreless main
Of Eternity, it sought again
The shelter and rest of the Isle of Time,
And knocked at the door of its house of pain!

On the tavern hearth the embers glow,
The laugh is deep and the flagons low;
But without, the wind and the trackless sky,
And night at the gates where a soul would go!

ON THE FLY-LEAF OF THE RUBAIYAT

Deem not this book a creed, 't is but the cry
Of one who fears not death, yet would not die;
Who at the table feigns with sorry jest.
To love the wine the Master's hand has pressed,
The while he loves the absent Master best,—
The bitter cry of Love for love's reply!

IN AN ALBUM

Like the south-flying swallow the summer has flown,
Like a fast-falling star, from unknown to unknown
Life flashes and falters and fails from our sight,—
Good-night, friends, good-night.

Like home-coming swallows that seek the old eaves,
Like the buds that wait patient beneath the dead leaves,
Love shall sleep in our hearts till our hands meet again,
Till then, friends, till then!

WITH APRIL ARBUTUS, TO A FRIEND

Fairer than we the woods of May,
Yet sweeter blossoms do not grow
Than these we send you from our snow,
Cramped are their stems by winter's cold,
And stained their leaves with last year's mould;
For these are flowers which fought their way
Through ice and cold in sun and air,
With all a soul might do and dare,
Hope, that outlives a world's decay,
Enduring faith that will not die,
And love that gives, not knowing why,

Therefore we send them unto you;
And if they are not all your due,
Once they have looked into your face
Your graciousness will give them place.
You know they were not born to bloom
Like roses in a crowded room;
For though courageous they are shy,
Loving but one sweet hand and eye.
Ah, should you take them to the rest,
The warmth, the shelter of your breast,
Since on the bleak
And frozen bosom of our snows
They dared to smile, on yours who knows
But that they might not dare to speak!

IMMORTALITY

My window is the open sky,
The flower in farthest wood is mine;
I am the heir to all gone by,
The eldest son of all the line.

And when the robbers Time and Death
Athwart my path conspiring stand,
I cheat them with a clod, a breath,

And pass the sword from hand to hand!

J. E. B.

Not all the pageant of the setting sun
Should yield the tired eyes of man delight,
No sweet beguiling power had stars at night
To soothe his fainting heart when day is done,
Nor any secret voice of benison
Might nature own, were not each sound and sight
The sign and symbol of the infinite,
The prophecy of things not yet begun.
So had these lips, so early sealed with sleep,
No fruitful word, life no power to move
Our deeper reverence, did we not see
How more than all he said, he was,—how, deep
Below this broken life, he ever wove
The finer substance of a life to be.

BY A GRAVE

Oft have I stood within the carven door
Of some cathedral at the close of the day,
And seen its softened splendors fade away
From lucent pane and tessellated floor,
As if a parting guest who comes no more,—
Till over all silence and blackness lay,
Then rose sweet murmurings of them that pray,
And shone the altar lamps unseen before,
So, Dear, as here I stand with thee alone,
The voices of the world sound faint and far,
The glare and glory of the moon grow dim,
And in the stillness, what I had not known,
I know,—a light, pure shining as a star,
A song, uprising like a holy hymn.

DUALITY

Within me are two souls that pity each
The other for the ends they seek, yet smile
Forgiveness, as two friends that love the while
The folly against which each feigns to preach.

And while one barters in the market-place,
Or drains the cup before the tavern fire,
The other, winged with a divine desire,
searches the solitary wastes of space.

And if o'ercome with pleasure this one sleeps,
The other steals away to lay its ear
Upon some lip just cold, perchance to hear
Those wondrous secrets which it knows—and keeps!

LULLABY

O Mary, Mother, if the day we trod
In converse sweet the lily-fields of God,
From earth afar arose a cry of pain,
Would we not weep again?
(*Sings*) Hush, hush, O baby mine,
Mothers twain are surely thine,
One of earth and One divine.

O Mary, Mother, if the day the air
Was sweet with songs celestial, came a prayer
From earth afar and mingled with the strain,
Would we not pray again?

(*Sings*) Sleep, sleep, my baby dear,
Mothers twain are surely near,
One to pray and one to hear.

   O Mary, Mother, if, as yesternight
A bird sought shelter at my casement light,
A wounded soul should flutter to thy breast,
Wouldst thou refuse it rest?
(*Sings*) Sleep, darling, peacefully,
Mary, Mother, comforts me;
Christ, her son, hath died for thee.

CONTENTS